Published in 1995 by
Stoddart Publishing Co. Limited
34 Lesmill Road
Toronto, Canada M3B 2T6
Tel. (416) 445-3333
Fax (416) 445-5967

Stoddart Books are available for bulk purchase for sales promotions, premiums,
fundraising, and seminars. For details, contact the **Special Sales Department** at the
above address.

CBC logo used by permission

Canadian Cataloguing in Publication Data

Giono, Jean, 1895–1970
The man who planted trees
Translation of: L'homme qui plantait des arbres.
ISBN 0-7737-5733-3

I. Title.

PQ2613.I57H613   1995   843'.912   C95-930352-9

Printed and bound in Hong Kong

*Stoddart Publishing gratefully acknowledges the support of the Canada Council, Ontario
Ministry of Culture, Tourism, and Recreation, Ontario Arts Council, and Ontario Publishing
Centre in the development of writing and publishing in Canada.*

THE MAN WHO PLANTED TREES

A story by Jean Giono
Translation by Jean Roberts
Illustrated by Frédéric Back

Stoddart

The exceptional qualities in a man's character reveal themselves only when one has the opportunity to study him over a period of many years. If he is utterly unselfish, shows unparalleled generosity, has never sought material gain and in addition has left the world a visibly changed place, then without doubt one has encountered a truly memorable character.

About forty years ago I set out on a walking tour, high in the Alps, in a region quite unknown to travellers, where these ancient mountains thrust down into Provence.

The area is bounded to the south and southeast by the Durance as it flows between Sisteron and Mirabeau, to the north by the river Drôme from its source as far as the town of Die and to the west by the plains of Comtat Venaissin and the foothills of Mont Ventoux.

It is made up of sections of three different districts: the northern part of the Basses-Alps, the southern portion of the Drôme, and a small triangle of the Vaucluse.

la Drôme

Die

Valdrôme

Serres

le Buëch

Chalançon

Rémuzat

Sisteron

Salérans

la montagne de Lure

Brantes

Sédevon

la Durance

le mont Ventoux

Banon

Manosque

My trek began at twelve or thirteen hundred metres above sea
level, on barren moors through a bleak, monotonous landscape
where nothing grew but wild lavender.
The route led across this region at its widest point, and after
hiking for three days I found myself in a dreary wasteland,
desolate beyond description. I made camp near the remains of an
abandoned village and, my supply having run out the day before, I
had to find water.

The cluster of houses, although in ruins reminding me of an old wasps' nest, made me think that once there must have been a fountain there, or perhaps a well. There was indeed a fountain, but it was dry. The roofless houses eaten away by wind and rain, the chapel with its crumbling belfry, stood arranged like houses and churches in a living village, but here all life had vanished.

It was a June day with a bright sun in a cloudless sky but over these bare highlands there blew a fierce, insufferable wind. Growling through the skeletons of the houses it sounded like a wild beast disturbed in the devouring of its prey.
I felt I had to move camp.

After walking for five hours I still had found no water, and could see nothing that gave me hope of finding it. Everywhere I came upon the same drought, the same coarse weeds. Then in the distance it seemed to me that I saw a small dark silhouette. I took it for a solitary tree, but in any case made my way towards it.

It was a shepherd, and resting on the burning ground beside him lay about thirty sheep.

After letting me drink from his gourd, he presently led the way to his sheepfold in a hollow in the plain. He drew water, and excellent water it was, from a very deep natural well over which he had rigged a simple windlass.

The man spoke very little, which is often the way with people who live alone, but he appeared confident and quite sure of himself, which seemed somehow strange in this barren land.

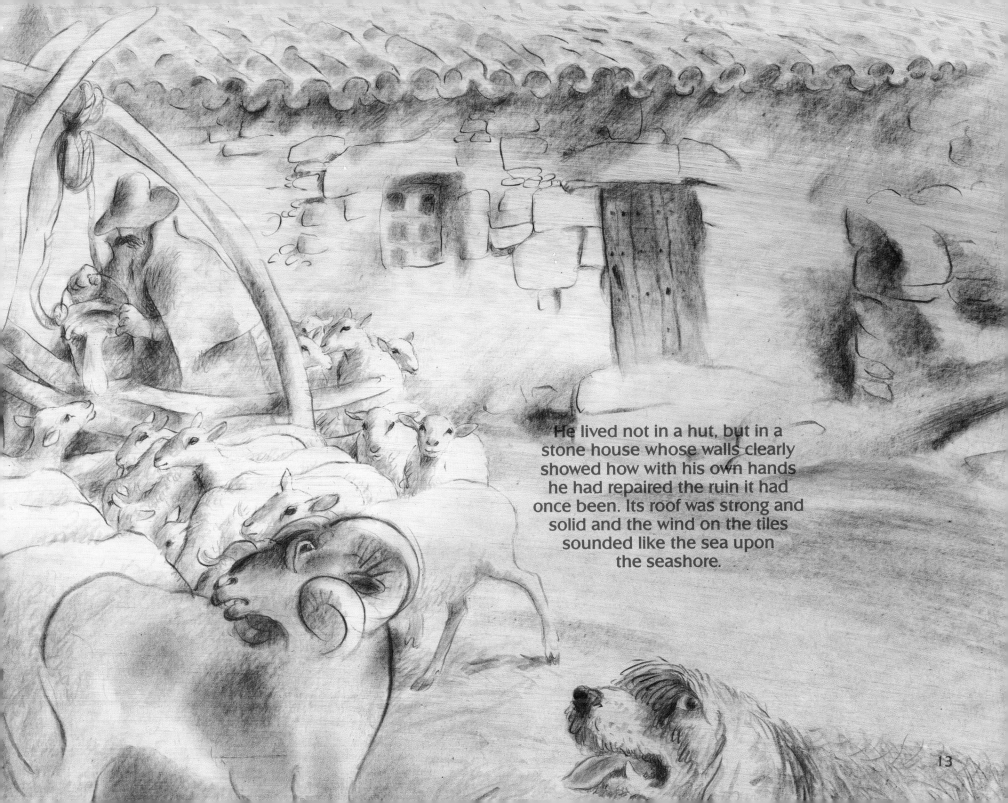

He lived not in a hut, but in a
stone house whose walls clearly
showed how with his own hands
he had repaired the ruin it had
once been. Its roof was strong and
solid and the wind on the tiles
sounded like the sea upon
the seashore.

13

Inside it was neat and tidy, dishes washed, floor swept, shotgun oiled; and his soup simmered over the fire. I noted that he was freshly shaved, that all his buttons were firmly sewed on, and that his clothes were darned with that meticulous care that makes the mend invisible.

He shared his soup with me and when I offered him my tobacco pouch he told me that he did not smoke. The dog, silent like his master, was friendly without fawning.

14

It had been agreed that I would spend the night there, as the nearest village was still almost two days' walk away. Villages in this region were few and far between, and besides I knew well what they were like: four or five of them were scattered over the slopes of these highlands, each one at the very end of a cart-track, among copses of white oaks. They were inhabited by charcoal burners. The living was poor and families, huddled together in a climate which was very harsh both in summer and in winter, found no escape from the neverending conflict of personalities. The constant longing to escape grew into a crazed ambition.

15

Endlessly the men carted their charcoal to town, then returned home. Even the most stable characters crack under such a relentless grind. The women seethed with resentment; there was rivalry in everything — from the sale of charcoal to the price of a church pew. They were rivals in virtue and rivals in vice, and between vice and virtue a fierce battle raged incessantly.

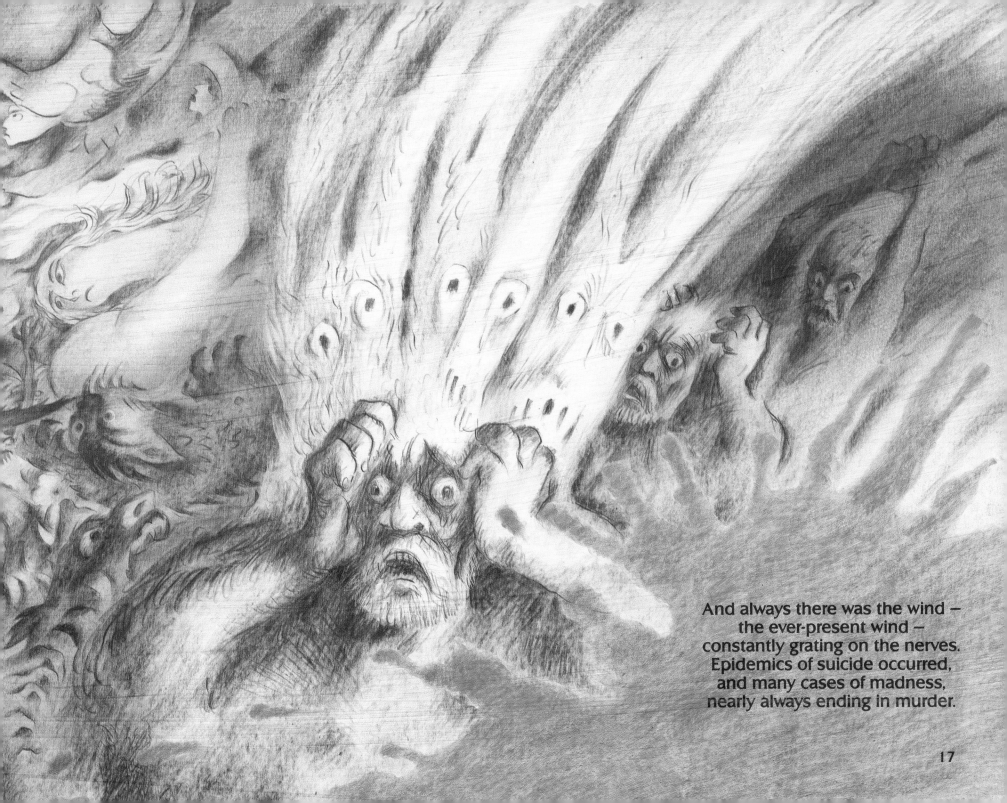

And always there was the wind —
the ever-present wind —
constantly grating on the nerves.
Epidemics of suicide occurred,
and many cases of madness,
nearly always ending in murder.

17

The shepherd went to fetch a little sack and onto the table he emptied a pile of acorns. He began to examine them very carefully, one by one, separating the good from the bad, while I sat smoking my pipe. I offered to help but he told me it was his work. Indeed, seeing how meticulously he carried out his task, I did not insist. That was the only time we spoke.

When he had set aside enough acorns, he divided them into piles of ten. As he did this he discarded the smaller ones or those that were cracked, for now he was examining them very, very closely indeed. When finally there lay before him a hundred perfect acorns, he stopped and we went to our beds.

Being in this man's company brought a great sense of peace, so the following morning I asked him if I might stay on and rest for the day. He seemed to find that quite natural, or rather, he gave me the impression that nothing could disturb him. The day of rest was not absolutely necessary, but I was intrigued and I wanted to learn more about him. He let his sheep out of the pen and led them to their grazing, but before he went, he took the little bag of carefully chosen acorns and soaked them in a pail of water. I noticed that for a walking staff he carried an iron rod, as thick as my thumb and about as high as my shoulder.

Pretending to take a leisurely stroll, I followed him at a distance, keeping on a parallel path with him. The pasture for his sheep was down in a dell. Leaving his dog in charge of the little flock he began to climb towards the place where I was standing. I feared he was coming to reproach me for my indiscretion, but I was wrong; it happened to be on his way and he invited me to join him if I had nothing better to do. He was going a little farther on, to the top of the hill.

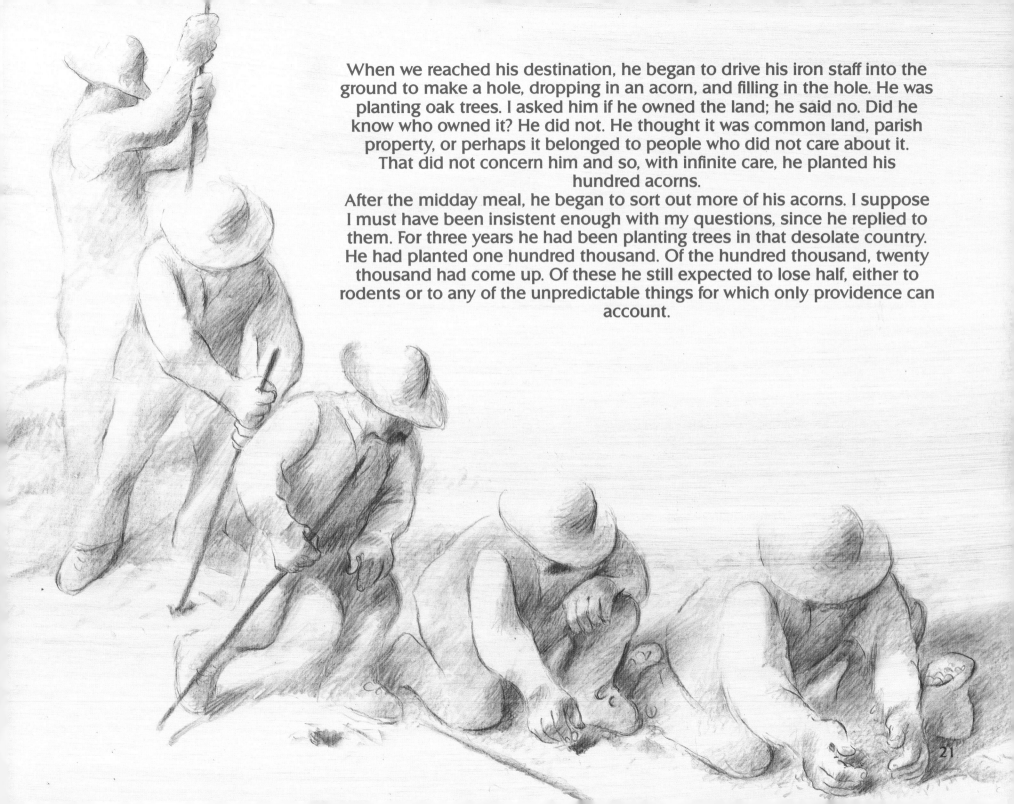

When we reached his destination, he began to drive his iron staff into the ground to make a hole, dropping in an acorn, and filling in the hole. He was planting oak trees. I asked him if he owned the land; he said no. Did he know who owned it? He did not. He thought it was common land, parish property, or perhaps it belonged to people who did not care about it. That did not concern him and so, with infinite care, he planted his hundred acorns.

After the midday meal, he began to sort out more of his acorns. I suppose I must have been insistent enough with my questions, since he replied to them. For three years he had been planting trees in that desolate country. He had planted one hundred thousand. Of the hundred thousand, twenty thousand had come up. Of these he still expected to lose half, either to rodents or to any of the unpredictable things for which only providence can account.

21

That left ten thousand oaks to grow on this tract of land where before there had been nothing. It was then that I wondered about the man's age. He was clearly more than fifty years old. Fifty-five, he told me, and his name was Elzéard Bouffier. He had owned a farm down in the lowlands, which had been his life.

There he had lost his only son and then his wife, and had withdrawn into this solitude where he was content to live quietly with his lambs and his dog. It was his opinion that the land was dying for lack of trees. He went on to say that he himself had nothing of importance to accomplish, so he had resolved to remedy this state of affairs.

Although I was young I too was leading a solitary existence at that time and felt I understood how to deal tactfully with reclusive spirits, but still I erred. Because of my youth, whenever I thought of the future I thought only of my own, my search for my own happiness and no one else's. So I said that in time those ten thousand oaks would be magnificent, but it would take thirty years.

He answered quite simply that if God were to grant him another thirty years of life he would have planted so many more that the present ten thousand would be like a drop of water in the ocean. Already he was studying the growth of beech trees, and had a nursery full of seedlings grown from beech nuts, which he protected from his sheep with a wire fence. They were quite beautiful. He was also thinking of birches for the dales, where he told me there was moisture just below the surface of the soil.

The next day we parted.

With the following year came the First World War, in which I was engaged for five years. An infantryman was hardly likely to have trees on his mind and, truth to tell, the whole encounter had not made much impression on me. I thought planting acorns was a hobby much like collecting stamps and had forgotten about it.

After demobilization, I found myself the possessor of a small gratuity and a great desire to breathe pure air. That was my one objective as I set off once more on the road to the barren lands.

The country had not changed; but in the distance beyond the deserted village I noticed a sort of greyish mist that lay on the hilltops like a carpet. The shepherd who planted trees had been in my mind since the day before. 'Ten thousand oak trees', I thought to myself, 'really need a great deal of space.'

I had seen so many people die in those five years it was easy to imagine that Elzéard Bouffier, too, was dead, especially since at twenty we think men of fifty are ancient, with nothing left to do but die. He was not dead, in fact he was more vigorous than ever. He had changed his occupation. He had kept only four sheep, but he now possessed over one hundred hives of bees. He told me, and I could see for myself, that the war had not disturbed him and he had continued his planting, unperturbed.

The oaks of 1910 were now ten years old and taller than either of us. It was such an impressive sight that I was struck dumb, and, as he never spoke, we spent the whole day in silence, walking through his forest. It was in three sections and measured eleven kilometres long and three kilometres at its widest. When I reminded myself that all this was the work of the hand and soul of this one man, with no mechanical help, it seemed to me that after all men might be as effective as God in tasks other than destruction.

He had followed his dream, and beech trees as high as my shoulder, stretching as far as the eye could see, were witness to it. The oaks were dense and strong enough to no longer be at the mercy of rodents. Indeed, had providence herself planned to destroy this man's creation, she would from now on have had to resort to cyclones.

He showed me handsome groves of five-year-old birches, planted in 1915, the year I was fighting at the battle of Verdun. They were set out in all the hollows, where he had guessed – and rightly – there was moisture near the surface. They were like adolescents, tender, yet sturdy and confident.

Nature, in turn, had just followed her natural cycle. He did not worry about it. Steadfastly he had gone about his simple task.

On the way down through the village I saw water flowing in streams which in living memory had always been dry. This was truly the most impressive example of nature's regenerative powers that I had ever seen. A long time ago these brooks had been full of water. Among the miserable villages I mentioned before some were built on the sites of ancient Roman settlements and archaeologists digging in the ruins had found fishhooks where in the twentieth century drought had made it necessary to use cisterns to ensure even a modest supply of water.

The wind too had scattered seeds abroad and as the water reappeared, so did willow trees, reeds, meadows, gardens, flowers, and a reason for living. The change had come about so gradually that it was simply taken for granted. Of course, hunters who climbed these heights in search of hares or wild boar had noticed the abundant growth of little trees, but had put it down to some caprice of nature. That is why no one meddled with the work of the shepherd. If they had suspected it was man's work they would have interfered. But who would even think of him?

Who in the villages or among the authorities could ever have imagined such constant, magnificent generosity?

Each year, from 1920 on, I paid a visit to Elzéard Bouffier. I never saw him lose heart, nor was he ever deterred. And often, God knows, it must have seemed that heaven itself was against him. I never tried to imagine his frustrations, but to achieve his aim he must have had to overcome many obstacles; to ensure the success of such a passion he must surely have battled with and overcome despair.

One year he had planted more than ten thousand maples,
every one of which had died. The following year he planted no
more maples and returned to beech trees, which did even
better than the oaks.
To properly appreciate this man's extraordinary qualities it
must be remembered that he lived and worked in solitude;
solitude so complete that towards the end of his life he lost
the habit of speech. Or was it that he saw no need for it?

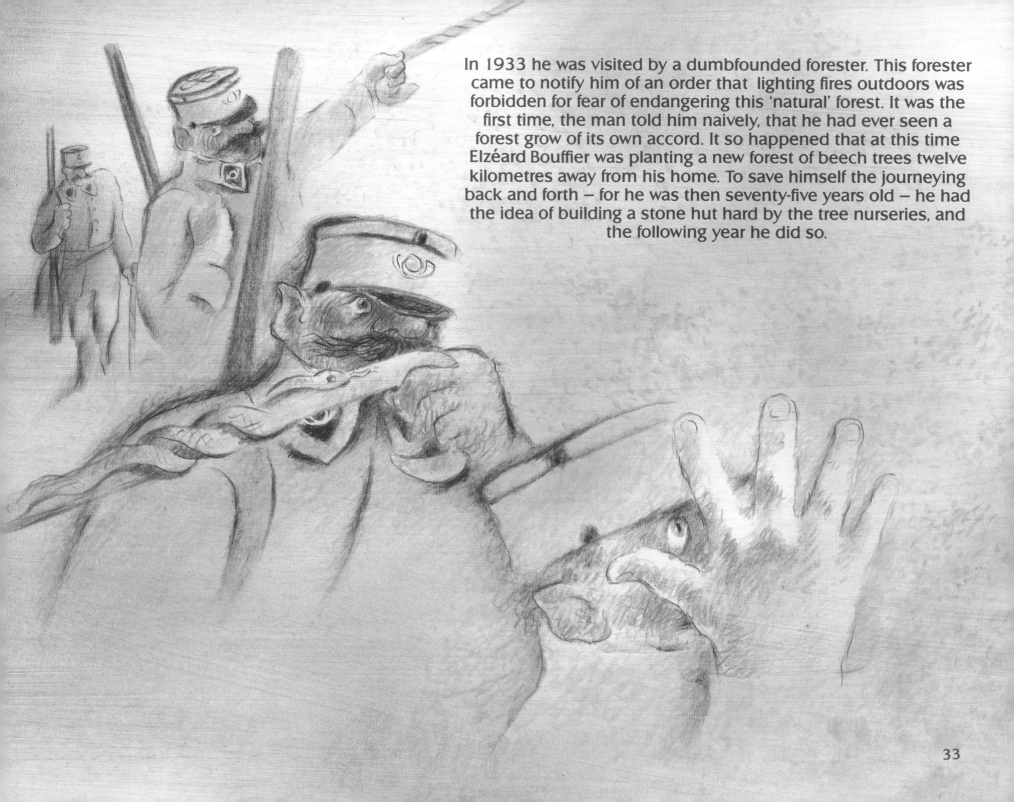

In 1933 he was visited by a dumbfounded forester. This forester came to notify him of an order that lighting fires outdoors was forbidden for fear of endangering this 'natural' forest. It was the first time, the man told him naively, that he had ever seen a forest grow of its own accord. It so happened that at this time Elzéard Bouffier was planting a new forest of beech trees twelve kilometres away from his home. To save himself the journeying back and forth – for he was then seventy-five years old – he had the idea of building a stone hut hard by the tree nurseries, and the following year he did so.

In 1935 a whole delegation of authorities arrived to inspect the 'natural forest': a high-ranking official from the Forestry Department, one elected Member of Parliament, a few technical experts. There was a great deal of useless talk. It was decided something must be done but, happily, nobody did anything – save for one useful thing: the forest was placed under government protection and charcoal burning was prohibited. You see, it was really quite impossible not to be enchanted by the beauty of these young, healthy trees. They had even cast their spell over the Member of Parliament.

One of the senior foresters in the delegation was a friend of mine and I explained the mystery to him. The following week we both set out in search of Elzéard Bouffier. He was hard at work, about twenty kilometres from the place where the official inspection had taken place.

I was right about my friend the forester. He had always been able to appreciate the important things in life, and he was a man who knew how to keep his own counsel. I offered the shepherd the few eggs I had brought as a present. The three of us shared our lunch and sat for several hours in silent contemplation of the landscape.

The slopes we had climbed on the way up were covered with tall trees about four times our own height, and I remembered how in 1913 it had looked quite desolate. Regular work in a peaceful atmosphere, brisk mountain air, the simple life and above all peace of mind, had endowed this old man with almost awe-inspiring health; he was one of God's athletes. How many more hectares, I wondered, would he cover with trees?

Before we took our leave, my friend made a small suggestion about the kind of tree which seemed to suit the soil here. He did not press the point. 'For the simple reason,' he told me afterwards, 'that this man knows more about it than I do.'

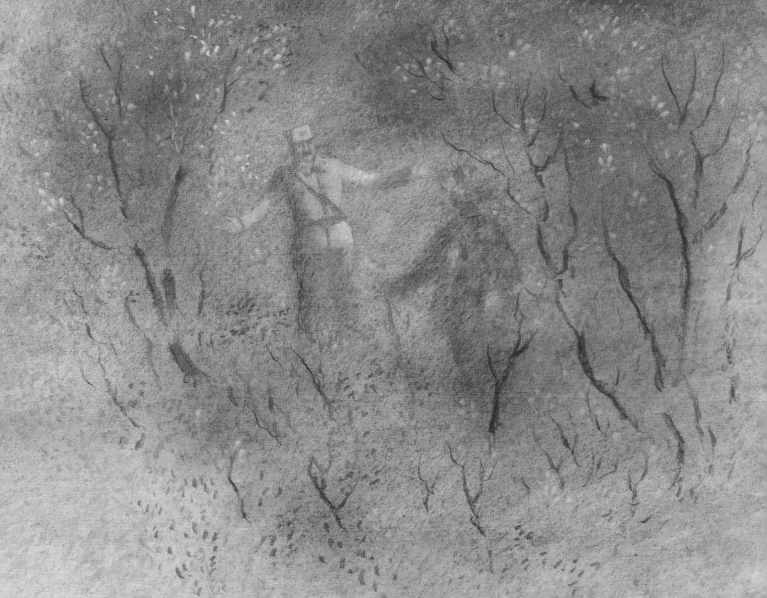

The thought must have been turning over and over in his mind, for after we had been walking for an hour he added: 'He knows more about it than anyone else in the world. He has found the perfect way to be happy.'

Thus, not only the forest but the happiness of Elzéard Bouffier was protected, thanks to this senior forester. He appointed three men to the task of guarding the woods, and intimidated them to such a degree that they resisted every kind of bribe the charcoal burners could offer.

The only serious danger to his work arose during the Second World War. Automobiles at this time were powered by wood-burning generators, for which there was never enough wood. Cutting was begun among the oaks of 1910, but they were so far from transportation routes that the whole enterprise proved financially unsound, and it was abandoned. The shepherd knew nothing of all this. He was thirty kilometres away, quietly going about his business, ignoring the war in 1939 just as he had ignored it in 1914.

I saw Elzéard Bouffier for the last time in June 1945. He was then eighty-seven. Again I had set out on the road to those barren moors but now, in spite of the disruption caused by the war, there was a bus which ran from the Durance valley up into the mountains. I decided it must be because of this relatively speedy means of transport that I could not recognize the places where my walks used to lead me, and it seemed that the route was taking us through new territory. It took the name of a village for me to realize that I really was in the region that was once deserted and in ruins.

The bus dropped me at Vergons.

In 1913 this hamlet of no more than a dozen houses had three inhabitants who set snares to make a living. They were wild creatures who hated each other and who were physically and morally not far removed from primitive man; surrounding them were the abandoned houses overrun with nettles.

They were beings without hope, death their only future — a condition that rarely inspires virtue.

40

Now everything was different – even the air itself!
Instead of the harsh, dry winds I remembered,
there blew a gentle breeze, filled with fragrance.
From the mountain tops came a sound like
rushing water; it was the wind rustling through the
forest. Then, even more astonishing, I heard the
sound of real water and saw that a fountain had
been built and was splashing merrily. What
moved me most of all was that beside it someone
had planted a linden tree, now about four years
old and already in full leaf. It was the perfect
symbol of rebirth.

Vergons showed further signs of the kind of labour that can only be inspired by hope, a hope that had been restored. Ruins were cleared away, crumbling walls torn down, and five houses rebuilt. The inhabitants of the hamlet now numbered twenty-eight, among whom were four young families. The new houses, freshly rough-cast, stood in kitchen gardens where flowers and vegetables grew in orderly confusion: roses and cabbages, snapdragons and leeks, celery and anemones. It was a place where from now on people would want to live.

From this point I continued on foot. The war had not been over long enough for life to reach its full flowering, but Lazarus had emerged from the tomb! On the lower slopes of the mountain I could see small fields of young barley and rye, and down in the narrow valleys a few meadows were turning green.

It has taken only eight years since that time for the whole countryside to glow with health and prosperity. Where I had seen ruins in 1913 there now stand clean, freshly plastered farmhouses, evidence of happy, comfortable lives.

Fed by the snow and rain which the forests now conserve, dried up springs have again begun to flow and their waters have been channelled. In the maple groves each farm has its own fountain brimming over onto carpets of fresh mint.

Bit by bit the villages have been rebuilt. People from down on the plains where land is expensive have come to settle, bringing youth, life and the spirit of adventure. Along the roads one meets healthy men and women, and boys and girls full of laughter; all have rediscovered the joys of a simple country life. Counting those who lived here in the old days, now quite changed by their new life in such peaceful surroundings, and including the newcomers, more than ten thousand people owe their happiness to Elzéard Bouffier.

48

When I consider that the physical and spiritual resources of just one human being were enough to turn a desert into the land of Canaan, I realize that in spite of everything mankind is admirable.

49

But when I think of all that it took to accomplish this work – the passionate determination, the steadfastness, the unfailing generosity of spirit – I am overcome with respect for that old, unlearned peasant who was able to carry out such a task, a task worthy of God.

Elzéard Bouffier died peacefully in the hospice in Banon in 1947.